Kaha the Kea

For all those people who are kaha enough to not always do what they are told. Kia kaha.
– Craig Smith

For my wife, Marguerite, without whom I would never have been illustrating children's books.
– Bruce Potter

First published in 2012 by Craig Smith Publishing
P.O. Box 330, Queenstown 9348, New Zealand

ISBN 978-0-473-21350-3

 'Kaha the Kea' the music was composed using a generic 12-bar rhythm and blues rundown. The songwriter believes that any similarities to other songs are coincidental.

National Library of New Zealand Cataloguing-in-Publication Data

Smith, Craig, 1972-
Kaha the Kea / Craig Smith ; illustrations: Bruce Potter.
ISBN 978-0-473-21350-3
1. Children's songs—Texts. [1. Kea—Songs and music. 2. Birds—
New Zealand—Songs and music. 3. Songs.]
I. Potter, Bruce (Bruce Anthony) II. Title.
782.42083—dc 23

12 11 10 9 8 7 6 5 4 3 2 1

Design by Book Design Ltd, www.bookdesign.co.nz
Kaha the Kea is printed using soy ink and FSC environmentally friendly paper.

Kaha the Kea

Words and music by **Craig Smith**
Illustrations by **Bruce Potter**

Kaha the Kea was

flying around.

He gnawed on my belt

and my trousers fell down!

Trip!!
Kea
Ha Ha Ha

I was upset
– my bare bottom
was getting wet.

But Kaha the Kea just laughed.

Kea aha ha ha ha

Kaha the Kea was flying to school,
flashing his colours and
trying to look cool.

All of his friends said,

"You look like
a fool, bro."

But Kaha the Kea just laughed.

AB'S
KAHA
RAP

Kea Kea

aha ha ha ha

Kaha the Kea liked shiny things,
landed on Mum's shoulder
and grabbed her earrings.

Mother yelled out,

"Oh you cheeky thing!"

But Kaha the Kea just laughed.

Kea Kea aha hahaha

Kaha the Kea flew very far,

and ripped all the rubber
from the windows of our car.

JIM 1

Dad yelled out,

"You naughty kea!"

But Kaha the Kea just laughed.

"You'll never catch me –
I'm so cheeky,
and I'm too clever."

Kea aha ha ha ha

screech!!

Tap
Tap

Kea Conservation Trust

One of a few native New Zealand parrots and the only alpine parrot in the world, the kea is unique. Over decades and mainly as a result of humans' actions, the number of kea has been reduced from a healthy population down to an estimated 1,000–5,000. (It is estimated that around 150,000 were culled in a government-sponsored programme that stopped in 1971.) While the kea is now endangered, organisations like the Kea Conservation Trust are telling the kea's story and showing how we can all help the kea population increase back to healthy levels once again.

www.keaconservation.co.nz

Want to continue the adventure with Kaha?

www.youtube.com. Search: Kaha the Kea Craig Smith

This fun and informative documentary for all ages, presented by Craig Smith, is a 12-minute educational resource so you can learn more about the kea.

Interactive e-book

www.craigsmith.co.nz/KahaTheKea/iPad.html

Link to the Apple App Store where you can download "Kaha the Kea for iPad", an interactive e-book loaded with animation and music!